The Awakening of the Gift

The Awakening of the Gift

ALDIVAN TORRES

Canary Of Joy

Contents

1

The Awakening of the Gift
Aldivan Torres
The Awakening of the Gift

Author: Aldivan Torres
©2020- Aldivan Torres
All rights reserved.

_____This book, including all its parts, is copyrighted and cannot be reproduced without the author's permission, resold or downloaded._

Aldivan Torres is a writer consolidated in several genres. So far, the titles have been published in dozens of languages. From an early age, he has always been a lover of the art of writing, having consolidated a professional career from the second half of 2013. He hopes, with his writings, to contribute to international culture, arousing the pleasure of reading in those who do not have the habit. Your mission is to win the hearts of each of your readers. In addition to literature, his main amusements are music, travel, friends, family and the pleasure of life itself. "For literature, equality, fraternity, justice, dignity and honor of the human being always" is his motto.

1-The Awakening

Co-vision's gone. Gradually, Renato and I will resume consciousness. Everything we'd lived through was nothing but a time-lapse revealing of mysteries that had not lasted more than thirty minutes.

After waking up, we greet each other moved by the beautiful story revealed. Would we have the same disposition and courage as the legendary Victor? Of course, the situations were entirely different. We were young of the 21st century, an early age of his more than his even with many challenges to fulfill.

Basically, if we could follow your example, surely victories would happen more easily. However, reiterating, the situations were incomparable.

At a quick meeting, we decided to return to the master's house This would be a good opportunity to expand our knowledge and ask for a safer guidance regarding how to continue.

Certainly, we advance, facing the same difficulties as ever, worlds with positive and motivating thought over the future of our venture Now all that remained was a head held high.

The full course was carried out in about half an hour at regular and steady steps We're finally here in front of the hovel, we stopped a little at this point, we were thrilled because we were about to find out what fate was reserving us or at least a forwarding which would be key to our double.

Instants later, we partially overcome our entrances. Once we realized the door was unlocked, we walked in without asking for permission because we already considered ourselves home.

We found the master. He was in the middle of the house, with his eyes closed to meditate. A little afraid, we approach him and touch him with the purpose of waking him up. Then he opens his eyes, sketches a smile and gets up. With a sign, he asks us to sit down and start a conversation.

"So? Did it work out with the co-vision technique?

"It was a wonderful thing. In a matter of seconds, a film was passed on in our minds. Very interesting indeed. It was worth it! (The psychic)

The Awakening of the Gift

"What now? What's the next step? (Renato)

"Inspiring in history revealed, you must also seek to achieve the great miracle: "The meeting of two worlds." This will only be possible if there's too much dedication on your part. (Angel)

"How's that going? (The psychic)

"The key to the question is in training. Find the healer in Carabais. He still lives in the painted site. In your experience, you must know the best way to reach the goal. My share is already fulfilled, and it was a success. Now I can rest in peace. It was nice meeting you. Aldivan and Renato, success on their walk. Keep it up all the time. You will still be proud of this state and country.

"Thank you for everything, master. We'll never forget him. (The psychic)

"We'll take your lessons forward. For right and fair! (Renato)

"One for all and one for all! (Angel)

"For the humble and wronged! Friends forever. (The psychic)

The emotion has taken over the moment. We got up. As we approach each other, our action resulted in a triple hug. For a moment, we feel the strength of our feelings, friendship. With our union, a small torch of fire came down from the sky, lighting the whole place. There, there was our star guide, who would help us in the hardest times. When the embrace ended, the torch went back to the place of origin. We're done saying goodbye. With tears in our eyes, we finally retreat from our benefactor. We've crossed the door. On the outside, we begin the walk to the village of Cimbres. A new stage in sight and that promised many emotions and discoveries. Keep following, readers.

From the beginning of the new journey, we kept at the disposal, claw, and courage from always similar to the first challenge than the mountain. Although they were different situations, the feeling was the same. Besides, precaution, patience, and tranquility were also cultivated because they were key to a possible success. Lesson learned during the road of life with the convivial with excellent masters. That included friends, family, spiritual advisors.

Everything could work out or not. The most important thing was learning and evolution achieved with every new experience. We become eternal apprentices. To achieve that, we would continue to carry on with our heads held high, growing values like dignity, friendship, simplicity, loyalty, and transparency. This was the brand of the dynamic duo of the series the psychic formed by the psychic and young Renato.

The saga continued. We're going through places we've known; we're pleased to relive various situations. Our imagination is in the line of time and space. How many feet didn't go through their full of expectations? The answer is countless. To stand out from the crowd, we needed an intense dedication to our projects. Something we didn't need, thank God.

Created as always in our cause and inspiring us in our ancestors, we increase the pace of steps. A few minutes later, we've already spotted the famous architecture of Cimbres. Now, we were exhausted by the efforts unearthed. But we were hoping it would work out.

With 500 more meters down, we finally have access to the main street. When we get to the Church of Our Lady of the Mountains, a self-filled pass. We give her signal and she stops. We're on board. As you had enough passengers, the departure for research is immediate.

All the way through, we have a chance to have a nice chat with the travel companions and with the driver named Balthazar who was very nice. We've talked a little of everything including general news, sports, music, religion, politics, and relationship in the total of thirty minutes' journey.

At the end of the race, we go down, say goodbye and pay for the ticket. We're waiting for another car to leave for Arcoverde. We'd be halfway, in the old Carabais, in the purpose of meeting a famous master of the past. He was the healer who was over a hundred years old. What would happen?

Thirty minutes later, five more passengers arrive and then the car finally leaves. This one made; we grow silence. We've enjoyed meditating a little and enjoying nature. Between stops, we spend another thirty minutes on the road.

The Awakening of the Gift

The car stops at the edge of BR 232, we go down and pay for the ticket. We had a mile of miles on our way to walk to the center of the village. Apart from the course to the painted site we didn't know about because we haven't met him yet.

We're starting the new walk. The curves climb made me remember a past not too far away and how nice it felt to taste. I share my memories with Renato, who listens closely and opinions.

Though I was a sage man, and he gives me valuable and secret tips. I also enjoy complimenting the disposition of helping me since you met me. Over time, we had become brothers and friends, accomplices and faithful journey mates. This was key to the success of our endeavor.

We're moving on. Completing exactly twenty-five minutes of the climb, we have access to the first houses. When we found the first person, we asked for information on the painted site and the healer's person.

It's about a young blonde, average height, pink faces named Jacqueline. Describe in detail how to get there. Since you were unoccupied, you offer your company.

We'll take it. We crossed the whole village and took a dirt road. Right at first, we make conversation with the girl with the intent to get to know each other better and spend a little time.

"What are you doing for the bands, miss? (The psychic)

"I work as a health agent for three days a week. In my spare time, I do housework. In my house, there are four people, me, my sister and my parents. And you? (Jacqueline)

"I'm a public official and in the spare hours, a beginner writer. I work on my projects with my assistant Renato. (The psychic)

"This. I'm a key piece in stories. (Declared proud Renato)

"All right! What kind of writing? (Jacqueline)

"Realistic Fiction. But I wish to write real stories too. Did you get any tips? (The psychic)

"No. I only know simple people. But trust God will provide. (Jacqueline)

"I believe you too. (Renato)

"So, let it be. Maktub! (The psychic)

"Is the doctor's house still far away? (Asked the impatient Renato)

"Not much. Why? (Jacqueline)

"I'm hungry. (Renato)

"Easy. Let's keep walking quietly. You can make yourself comfortable, Jacqueline? (The psychic)

"Thank you.

The conversation instantly stopped. We diverted right into the road and entered a beat verdict facing the dry floor, thorns, and branches of the nearby bushes. But since we were from the place we were used to.

Further ahead, the path spreads a little, and we're more comfortable. In the field of vision, a hovel comes. On the signal of Jacqueline, we're moving forward to him. In about five minutes, we've met at the door about to knock. However, before we did that, the door opens mysteriously. Inside, the figure of the elder, who despite age keeps strong and strong features beyond the peculiar way of dressing, leather shorts, lace shirts and sole sandals.

With one gesture, he starts the conversation:

"Jack, what are you doing here? What about these others? They look familiar.

"Hi! These are my friends, psychic, and Renato. They want to talk to you. (Jaqueline)

"I'm the grandson of Victor. (The psychic)

"And I'm your assistant. (Renato)

"How? I thought so. You look a lot like your grandfather. Welcome. (Healer)

"Thank you. I'm proud of it. Can we come in? (The psychic)

"Yes, of course. You want to come too, Jack? (Healer)

"No, I'm coming. I just came to accompany you. Even for everyone. (Jaqueline)

"See you later!

We're in the house. Accompanying the host, we settle in drums willing in circles at the center of the hovel. After initial silence, the conversation is finally resumed.

"Well, what brought you here, to this end of the world? (Healer)

"We came from an unequal adventure and our master told us to look for him. (The psychic)

"He's called Angel and said that with his help we can achieve the miracle which consistence in the meeting between two worlds. Is it really possible? (Renato)

The healer's face got stiffed. He stayed for a few static moments to think. In these moments we wished to be powerful telepaths to guess exactly what was going on in your mind.

"Since we weren't, we were silent to wait for your statement what happened right after.

"Anything is possible, my dear, to depend on the dedication. First, though, I wish to meet you a little more. (Healer)

"All right. My name is Aldivan Torres, also known as the psychic or the son of God. I'm a public official and a writer on the off hours. I come from two incredible adventures with my assistant Renato who have rented my first two titles: "Opposing Forces" "And the dark night of the soul" I'm on a third project and to get it done, I need your help. (The psychic)

"This. Like he said, I'm your friend and assistant. (Renato)

"I get it. I believe I can help you with your goals. Do you accept training? (Healer)

"Sure. Always. (The psychic)

"We're ready. (Renato complement)

"All right! For us to achieve success, you must remain here for seven days. As for the accommodations, don't worry. I have enough beds. (Healer)

"Thank you. Is that really necessary? (The psychic)

"Yes. Put your shyness aside and be my guest. Your grandfather wasn't like that. (In laughter, the healer)

"I don't think he's got a way. (Renato)

"Good, I'll sleep now. If you're hungry, you can go to the kitchen and prepare something. Training starts tomorrow. (Healer)

"Roger that. (The psychic)

"You can be my guest, master. (Renato)

The healer stood up, stretched and tiresome came near one of the beds. He lay down and immediately fell asleep. Renato and I settled in, we exchanged ideas, and as predicted, we're hungry.

We go to the kitchen and make a quick snack. Thereafter, we left the hovel on a walk around. Three hours later, we came, and we found the awake master. We talked a little more, and we're available to help with housework. When we're done, we've performed other study and leisure activities.

With the arrival of the night, we had dinner and went out a little to contemplate the stars. With your experience, the healer gives us some astronomy lessons besides telling some interesting stories of his past.

We've been in this exercise for three hours. When it gets a little late, the healer retires. Since we had nothing to do, we followed him. The other day would be the beginning of a new journey, headed towards the unknown. What fate would reveal itself before us? Were we prepared for what came? These and other unanswered questions were about to be solved. Let's continue the saga of number three.

Fear of God

It's dawn. The sun rises, the birds sing and a soft breeze overcomes the wall flooding the whole environment. In a few moments, we wake up, we crawl, we'll take a shower. In the end, we went to the kitchen and with the host, we prepared breakfast with what we had available in the pantry.

We've taken the opportunity to narrow our ties until recent. When the food is ready, we sit at the table, and we serve ourselves in a communion ritual.

We feed in silence and respect. When we're done, we start a conversation in a way to direct doubts.

"When do we start our training? (The psychic)

"First, I want to know how Angel trained them. (Healer)

"I'll explain. We passed the test of development of the Holy Spirit gifts. It was six steps total. With them, we could develop a new technique, the co-vision that provided us with the first step vision. (Renato)

"I see. We must then continue on this line of reasoning until it reaches the top of the second stage. What was the gift left? (Healer)

"Was the fear of God". (The psychic)

"We'll start from there. Follow me. (Healer)

We obey the master by heading out. We've overstepped all obstacles. Out of the way, we've been running a verdict in the same way. Ten minutes later, walking vigorously, we entered a clearing. At the master's signal, we sat in the center of it. From then on, he starts explaining. Brought them here for a healthy debate. A trade of experiences, for there is no one in this world so wise that can't learn or anyone so ignorant that can't teach. Everyone, very or very, has luggage. (Healer)

"I agree. Life is characterized by a continuous process of teaching and learning, a very used term in education. (The psychic)

"The teacher said! But tell us, master, what have you to tell us about the gift of God. (Renato)

"From experience, unlike most people think, God doesn't want us to be afraid of him. It requires respect, dedication to its cause, following its laws and practical works in exchange for your love and protection. However, even those who insist on their mistakes, who are sunk in their darkened night" are not abandoned by the divine. This happens because he's a father first, and he's good with everyone. This consists of perfection. What about you? What concept do you have of this gift? (Healer)Look, master, in the period I was immersed in my dark night of the soul, I could have the dimension of two opposites of God, mercy and justice. At this time, I was totally carried away by my messenger, coming to think of owning the world. That's when the forces of good acted and imposed me their strength. They opened my eyes, punished me, and then I realized the evil I did. However, despite the insistent requests of my enemies, instead of convicting me, God freed me and resuscitated not just this time, but countless times. God is a father. The only condition that imposes us is a commitment to not repeating the same mistakes. In short, for all I've lived, I can conclude that we must grow the fear of God. We must not light your wrath, for your hand is too heavy for us mortals and fair. Beyond justice, there is mercy. This one is only achieved in case we earn your trust. We must have attitude and position. (I, the psychic)

"Despite my little age, I have something to tell you too. Ever since my mother passed away, my father treated me hard. From him, I learned about fear. We shouldn't let this control us. We need to dictate our actions. Being an author of your story. This was my experience of a human father. When I ran away, I found the mountain guardian and with her, I had a more dignified life. I could study, have friends, play and work, too. I found out with her teachings and investigating in books, a real father. A father who doesn't strike, who loves, who accepts us as we are, a truly human father. Fear, to me, is a father-son relationship. Like any relationship, you need debate, knowledge, complicity, fidelity, and loyalty. It's the only way it becomes complete. But we must never be afraid. It keeps us from God. (Renato)

"Splendid! Different opinions, but all meaningful. I've noticed the strong influence of personal experiences in your opinions. This is normal. I think we can try. (Healer)

"Try what? (The psychic)

"I also have the same doubt. (Renato)

"Complete the first cycle, the seven gifts. With proper lighting, we can absorb knowledge and make sure that way to continue to achieve a complete goal. (Healer)

"All right. We can try. (The psychic)

"How do we act? (Renato)

"Get up and form a circle. (Healer)

We obey the master. We hold hands and close the circle. Immediately, he kneels, prays softly and asks us to go through memory the previous challenges. In a matter of seconds, we reminisce the most remarkable moments of adventure to the present moment. Prayer finished, the master rises, and raises with ours, hands to heaven. Suddenly, the world trembles, darkens, and tongues like fire come down on our heads.

From there, we enter complete ecstasy. We are filled with the power from above similar to what happened to the apostles of Christ. That's about two thousand years ago.

This wonderful moment lasts only thirty seconds. When the fire languages are finished, we meet again just the three of us. The master then takes the word.

"I got it. I know the way to go. Shall we? (Healer)

"Could you give us a hand? (The psychic)

"No. Every day your concern. Let's go home. (Healer)

"All right. Shall we, Renato? (The psychic)

"Sure. (Renato)

Our trio began to go back and the questions kept coming into our minds. What would happen? Whatever it was we thought we were ready to face it because we had experience in challenges.

For now, the master was right, there was nothing to worry about. The first step has been taken. Now all that remained was race, courage, without fear and shameless to be happy.

With a little dedication and luck, we could get to the desired results. But this was the future.

While this one didn't arrive, we kept walking. About the same time as the trip, we arrived at the hovel. During the rest of the day, we'd be involved in other activities that had nothing to do with the challenge.

At night, we'd learn more about the universe and trade experiences. The master would plan the next steps and live the expectation of the next day that promised many new things.

When we were tired, we'd rest. It was usually early because in the place there weren't many entertainment options.

Keep following, readers.

The value of friendship

Night usually works. The dawn passes and dawn then. At the first light of the sun, we awaken. Immediately each of you will occupy in an activity the master will prepare breakfast while me and my faithful fellow adventures will take a bath.

In thirty minutes, we fulfill the obligation. We went to the room and changed our clothes. All right, let's go to the kitchen. Once we get there, we serve ourselves and the master takes advantage of himself.

Meanwhile, Renato and I exchanged classified information. But we don't have much time for this because in less than ten minutes the master will return. He sits with us at the table and politely waits for us to finish, so he can pronounce himself what doesn't take long.

"Did you sleep well? (Healer)

"Other than some nightmares, all right. (Inform Renato)

"Normal. Just a little anxious. (Confessed, the psychic)

"All right! Then we'll get started. With the lighting I had yesterday, I thought it'd be best to continue the training of the same way I started. A conversation with total freedom, respect, and interaction. Agreed? (Healer)

"It's okay. (The psychic)

"It's an interesting method. What are we going to talk about? (I wanted to know Renato)

"Today's theme is friendship. It contains a little of your trajectory and experience in this sense. (Healer)

"I'll start. Friendship to me, that's all. I learned this from the higher spirits, my family, friends, acquaintances, coworkers, spiritual masters and life. On this path, I loved, I suffered, I cried, I missed, I hit, I fought, and I got confused. But I got over it and forgave it. Anyway, I learned, I thought, and I want to keep on going after all. (The psychic)

"My beginning of history, as you know, is a little tragic. I only knew the good feelings when I met the guardian. She's my benefactor. That's when I had a greater contact with society. In them, there are schoolmates and my dear fellow adventure. (Renato)

"Thank you. (The psychic)

"What would you do for a needy friend? (Healer)

"It depends. If he was confused, I'd advise him. If you were in trouble, we'd try together, find a solution. In short, I'd help whatever was necessary. (The psychic)

"I'd put myself at your disposal at good times and bad times. (Explained Renato summarily)

"I like it. It would help, too. In this world, we're all the same. What we bring with concrete is good deeds. Money, pride, vanity, sorrows, disputes and selfishness lead to nothing. However, it is still very common to hear from false friends when you need the following sentence: "Not my problem." (Healer)

"Exactly. It's happened to me a lot. But I'm not like them. I will not repeat this mistake. (The psychic)

"Good! Even without much experience, I've seen cases of people who revolted and started acting the same way. (Renato comment)

"Never do that. Even if the blood boils, don't mix with this category of people. We need to get values and not share. (Healer)

"Jesus is the example. (The psychic)

"He's the main one. Mother Teresa of Calcutta, Sister Dulce, Zilda Arns, Dorothy Stang, Mother Paulina, Francisco Xavier, Santa Rita of Cassia, Nelson Mandela, Francis Of Assisi, Gandhi, among thousands of examples. (Healer)

"I've heard of it. They were wonderful. (Renato)

"Is it possible to reach their level of evolution, master? (The psychic)

"Don't compare yourself to anyone. Each has its peculiar history. The important thing is to grow good values, have experiences that life provides, have good companies, live and not be ashamed of being happy as music says. Time teaches. (Healer)

"I get it. I'll follow them. (The psychic)

"With my help, we can continue to mark history and charm hearts in the series of the psychic. (Renato)

"This. Follow fate with claw, strength, and faith that success will come as a consequence. Don't forget about me and the others. That's what friendship is. (Healer)

"Of course not. We value our origins. (I, the psychic)

"How about a hug? (Renato)

The emotion took over us all, and we accepted young Renato's suggestion. We're up. When you get close, the triple hug happens to last a few moments. There was a trio battling, seeking knowledge. Though they belonged to different worlds, they were united by fate. Every step of the way, the revealing meeting was approaching.

Finished the hug, we walked away. The master says goodbye, explaining he had chores to do in the village. When you leave, it's just the two of us. We have the idea to fix the hovel. Although it wasn't much of our beach, only good intention was valid.

When the master returned, we would continue to help him in other activities until the day are over. One more step has been accomplished. With the healer's experience, great lessons had stayed. Let's move on.

Complicity

A new day comes with the usual features. At some point, a cold wind hits our bodies already recovered from the previous efforts causing us to wake up. Immediately, I gather enough courage and strength to lift. I try one, two, three, four times. I'll catch up with the success last time.

In addition, I watch my adventure companion closely. I see that despite awake, my fellow adventure has not yet been disposed of at least effort. So, I decide to approach and fondly help you take an initiative. Five minutes later, both are already standing up.

In a quick conversation, we share the chores, and we'll be done. This one made, Renato and I prepared breakfast by exercising our cooking gifts. Meanwhile, the master takes his bath quickly. When you finish this task, change your clothes and meet us still in the kitchen.

When it comes to the environment, it still gives him time to suggest some improvements on the plate that at the time it's made of couscous with a bubbly cooked macaroon. We appreciate the help, and we'll give the final touch on the meal.

With everything ready, we serve ourselves and sit at the table while we eat, we start a friendly conversation.

First, I want to thank you for all the attention and dedication to our cause. But I still have some doubts left. Could you sanction them? (The psychic)

The Awakening of the Gift

"It depends. You'll get all the answers you need in time. The nerves and anxiety are just in the way. (Healer)

"It's not extraordinary. I want to know how many stages we have to perform and how to achieve the most desired miracle. (The psychic)

"Like I said, it'll be seven days of training. In this period, I request full focus on your part. The rest will come as a consequence. (Healer)

"All right. I'll wait. Any questions, Renato? (The psychic)

"Besides yours, I'm curious to know the true name of our worthy master. (Renato)

"You're asking too much. My baptism name is Secret. For now, stick to training and not silly things. (SCREAMS THE MASTER)

"All right. Sorry for the nerve. (Renato)

"Don't worry. Finish feeding. (Healer)

The master's voice sounded serious and firm. That makes us disciples take the request as order! Quietly, we continue to taste food very slowly. We ate a portion of each and since we were still feeling hungry, we repeat the dose.

Twelve minutes later, we're finally satisfied. When we're finished, we head to the improvised bathroom, so we can take care of our body. One at a time. Between bathing, change clothes and back to the kitchen we spent more forty minutes of our precious time. However, despite the delay, we find the radiant master and once again willing to help us.

"Can we get started? (Healer)

"Yes. (Me and Renato)

"Well, the subject approached today is complicity. Could you share your experiences in that sense? (Healer)

"Sure. I can say, undoubtedly, that this is one of my principal features. In any relationship it's critical. For example, in difficulties, we seek support. We're looking for someone to trust and share the weight of responsibilities. In case we don't find it, life gets a little emptier and sadder. Complicity and trust are two important links. (The psychic)

"I agree. We must also be as careful as we can so that we can deposit our trust in the right people. (Renato)

"All right! Renato. But it's hard at first to have this ability of judgment. Precaution must be the key word and knowledge is something necessary. Only with him is possible to decide. (Alerted the master)

"Have you ever had disappointments, master? (Renato)

"Too many. It's part of the process of evolution. The important thing is not to repeat the same mistakes. (Healer)

"Good point. I've also lived something similar over and over again. Mistakes make the way to the right. (I've been pushing)

"Exactly, my dear. Congratulations. I believe you will soon harvest the fruits of your work. They always persist. (Healer)

"I get it. Thanks again. (Renato)

"You're welcome. We'll take care of the household chores? (Healer)

"Yes. (Both of us)

We'll take the necessary material and start the suggested activity. When we're done, we'd do other pertinent jobs. The most important thing was that we're progressing in sight. Heading to success!

Reflections.

The other day, we performed the morning's correctional activities as usual and as we finished eating breakfast we met at the center of the hovel by the master's nomination. We sit on the floor next to each other. Thereafter, a moment finally the healer takes the initiative.

"Well, we're here again on the fifth day of training. Are you enjoying it so far? (Healer)

"I am. But I must confess to waiting for something more spectacular with incredible techniques, mysteries to be solved and extraordinary revelations. (The psychic)

"It's been a great learning for me. I have nothing to complain about. (Renato)

"I get it. Seer, it's normal for someone like you, with a great experience in adventure to expect this concept. But believe me, we'll have more concrete results acting this way. We need to do the information exchange. As for you, Renato, feel free. (The master)

"Thank you. (Renato)

"What's the next step? (The psychic)

"We'll talk today of a complex and universal theme, love. What are your opinions? (Healer)

"In love, I've tried everything." I felt the spiritual love of God, of delivery and complete resignation. Besides, I felt human love. It's something that involves attraction, approach, faith and convicted strength. However, regarding this last one, my experiences were not good. (The psychic)

"For my little age, I have experienced family love and passion is not too deep. As you know, my life has not been easy. (Renato)

"We understand Renato and admire him. In time, you'll have a chance to know true love. As for you, psychic, not discouragement. Happiness will come to you in the right time. The most important thing is to persevere in the fight to be happy because, in fact, that's what really matters. (Advised the healer)

"I hope so. And you? What are your experiences regarding love? (The psychic)

"Well, like any human being who's lived over a hundred years, I know a little of life. However, my spiritual work and the relationship with nature have always come in the first place. In a way, it kept me from people. That's it. We live on choices and mine were well thought. I don't regret it. (Healer)

"I agree. Making choices is the main act to become the main actors on the stage of our lives. Being a leader of yourself is the main goal. (The psychic)

"Let the consequences come! (Renato complement)

"This is exactly what I want to pass to your disciples. I wish from the bottom of my heart that they have the courage and strength to make their decisions and face them without fear of contradicting the greatest who support a false moral in our society. Be like the legendary Victor and his group of vigilantes who have marked history at an even harder time than the present. (Healer)

"We promised to try this way. (The psychic)

"Together, we can get the miracle, the so-awaited find between two worlds. (Declared with optimism, Renato)

"This is the way to talk. I like to see it. Any more observations? (Healer)

"No. What about you, Renato? (The psychic)

"Neither do I. (Renato)

"All right! Today's work is over here. I'll go out for a while, visit some friends in the village. You guys take care of home and think about our conversation. (Healer)

"All right. See you. (The psychic)

"See you later. (Renato)

"A hug. See you in a bit. (Healer)

That said, the master walked away, opened the door and left. Now it was just me and Renato. We'd take the master's advice. When he came back, he'd be proud of us because dedication and commitment would not miss our part. Let's continue our saga then.

Mediumship

One more day has passed. After we got up, tighten up, shower, eat breakfast and brush our teeth, we reunited with the healer. This one made, we settled in the bed located in his room. After locking the doors, the master had the safety needed to start the conversation.

"Well, ready?

"We always are. (The psychic)

"I believe so. (Renato)

"I thought about it a little. I've come to the conclusion that you make needed now the use of two techniques. Today, I'll teach you the first technique. It's about the improvement of medium. (Inform the healer)

"Very nice. Despite the various experiences I've had, I'm not fully developed. (Confessed, the psychic)

"Interesting. I have no experience. But in my case, is it possible? Even though I don't have a specific gift. (Renato)

"Answering both of you, you're never fully prepared. We're all high-level psychics. The question is how to prepare properly for these beyond life contacts that often save us from great dangers. I have one of the keys to reach this. (Healer)

"We're all listening closely. (I've prepared)

"Go ahead, master. (Ratified Renato)

"We've been living for six days and I've realized your ability and value. First, they gave me confidence and for this I will reveal to you one of my secrets. Listen up. (Healer)

The master stood up and approached the walls. Specifically, from one of the paintings nailed with very good taste. He took it out, leaving the show a mirror, the one we had visualized in the history of Victor.

With a signal, he asks for our approach. Once we get close, he'll come back to us.

"Close your eyes and concentrate on infinity. With this in mind, just once in the mirror.

We obey once more. When we feel prepared, we play simultaneously the mirror. Now, we enter into a kind of transcend our spirits overcome the various existing dimensions: we pass through the heavens, hell, the city of men, purgatory, limbo, abyss, dimensional doors, planets of the entire universe.

The experience is excellent and fast. Forty seconds, we're back on consciousness. When we woke up, we left the mirror. We're back to sitting while the master next to us seems anxious and restless. Let's start the dialogue again.

"This is wonderful! I've never felt so light and loose. It's like my senses are at the bottom of my skin, without any communication barrier.

"I felt something like that, too. Although they are a different world than ours, this technique shows how possible the encounter is, even though it's so desperate realities. (Renato)

"Glad you understood. As long as they have access to the second technique, they can complement this one, they will have the opportunity to achieve the miracle they so desire. It will be the opportunity for a reassess of life giving the opportunity to stipulate new goals and consolidate the already achieved. Anyway, a new walk that will be long if God wants. (Healer)

"That's great! Let's get on with the work, shall we, Renato? (The Son of God)

"Sure. But now I'm hungry. Can we prepare something? (Renato)

Renato's naivety provoked laughter at me and the master. What a character. Without him, the series the psychic wouldn't have the same charm he has.

"When we control ourselves, we start talking again.

"All right. Shall we go, master? (The psychic)

"Be my guest. For today, no more training. But don't forget to clean up the mess. (Healer)

Right away, we get up from the bed. We took a few steps, we opened the door and moved towards the kitchen. Once we got there, we started making a scramble of rice and beans seasoned with what we had available. In ten minutes, we'll finish prepping. Even though I'm not hungry, I'm following Renato into the tasting of this delight which I specialize in.

During the feeding, we share experiences and expectations. What was expecting us from now on? Would our effort be rewarded? What good would we take from this adventure for the rest of our lives? These and other questions would soon be answered in such a desired meeting.

While the time was not right, we'd be able to refuel. At the end, we begin other everyday activities. Forward, always! For readers and the universe so unique that it provided gifts! Forward.

The secret of the seven doors

The seventh day of experiences and internal fights carried out in the cottage of the mysterious healer, in the company of the same and Renato. Early, we rise at a frenetic rhythm and perform the usual activities in a record time.

"I'm done with breakfast; I don't contain my nerves and anxiety. I start because, the conversation with the others.

The Awakening of the Gift

"What now, master? Could you guide us in definitive? (The psychic)

"Already? Are you really ready? (Healer)

"I believe so, and what about you, Renato? (The Son of God)

"I'm with you, my friend. Let's move on. (Renato)

"Brave of you. You know, though, what are you up against? (Healer)

"No. But it doesn't matter much. What's life worth without adventures or meaningless? In my opinion, a total void. (The psychic)

"Explain it to us, master. (Renato requested)

"I like it. The next challenge is a big secret I've never revealed to anyone. Only if they do, they'll have a chance of achieving the wished miracle. You guys up for it? (Healer)

"What exactly is this about? (Renato)

"I usually call it a secret of the seven doors. It's several overlapped dimensions and every minute the situation gets even more complicated. If they fail, they can be trapped in one of their parallel dimensions. What do you say? (Healer)

"Excuse me, Renato, as leader of this venture I decide you'll stay out of this stage. Don't get me wrong, it's just that I have a greater experience in extreme situations. I'd rather continue only from now on. All right? (The psychic)

"I didn't understand you very well, but I do. (Renato)

"Excellent. What shall I do, master? (The psychic)

"First, follow me (Healer)

I obeyed the master and along with him, we followed to the room. We passed the door and locked it. When we're absolutely alone, we'll be communicating again.

"Close your eyes. (Asked the healer)

Even though I thought it was strange, I obeyed again. About thirty seconds later, I hear your voice again and this one's asking me to open them. In doing so, I have a stunning vision of a portal ahead of us and in my eyes of doubt the master is about to pronounce himself.

"Here is the gate of knowledge created by me. I'm one of the few in the land capable of it. He's like an enlarged reality. Open the door, pray to your guardian angel and overtake the obstacles. At the end, you'll find your way out.

"When can I go? (The psychic)

"Now. Hurry, because there's a time limit. (Inform the healer)

"All right. (The Son of God)

I start taking the first steps and even though I fight my fears continue to go on and on. I'll pull over. Furthermore, I'll stop for five seconds and breathe. When I'm done with this time, I'm grabbing the handle, I open the door, I take two steps and I close it behind me. What I see at first makes me impressed.

I'm in a flat, dark, extensive, and totally cryptic place. In a moment, the sky and the ground disappear and my body starts floating in the air helped by my secret techniques. I begin then, without definite direction. In time, I'm tired of myself, I'm thinking by asking for assistance from the higher forces that follow me and as an answer, a mysterious voice says that everything is about to begin. Trust that, for a little while and rest, supposed to be in the air. Next thing I know, I hear a ribbon echoing and pairs of lights and powerful shadows coming closer. With the experience, I have of the spirit plan, I realize the presence closer to them, which are the seven spirits of God. But what was the plan that carried them? To what end? Flying at the speed of light, they quickly arrive and surround me completely: are seven angelic warriors of the highest hierarchy, with their pairs of amazing wings, swords, spears, and stars ready for combat. Immediately, I'll be in telepathic contact with the same. I'm successful because a conversation begins soon.

"What do you want from me? (I, the psychic)

"We've come to prove your faith. To move on, you'll have to beat us in a fight. (Speaking of Miguel, the boss)

"Excuse me? (I asked incredulous)

"This is human. What you want is beyond the possibility for mortals, and we request from God this proof. (Lucifer, the Black Archangel)

"I get it. But shouldn't you be taking care of the humans? I don't understand the point of this fight. (The psychic)

"We are light and darkness in a total of seven. Together we are the divinity. We decided this because this is a sacred place you dared to penetrate. (All in choir)

"But don't worry. Since you are the son of God, can easily defeat us. (Lucifer laughs)

"The other holy ones laughed and their voices looked like thunder riff. What would now be the son of God? He's resolved to answer.

"In that plan, I'm just a human. But what you don't know is that I left God in spirit. There were many reincarnations on planet Earth for millennia and finally in this I got contact with the father. Today we are one because God is present in every innocent child, in every devoted mother and father, in orphans, in the poor and wronged of this world. Jesus is the example, for he was the first human to have the courage to say that God is a father. Which is a great truth because everyone who follows his law is their children regardless of creed, sexual option, religion or social position. God is the meeting of good hearts and even though it's just a poor human I know it. (I claimed)

"Blasphemy! Finish him. (Incited Lucifer)

My attitude incited the wrath of the archangels, and they're all over me. However, I didn't care. He'll unwind and respond to the prosecution. And that it was what God wanted.

At the moment the swords were ready to hit me in half, a shield protected me and rid me of the attacks. Soon the thunder laughed, filled the environment and the world shivered.

By my side was my spiritual guide. At his signal, everyone knelt down. Immediately, we feel the presence of the living God.

Since we were inferior beings, we couldn't see him just listen to him. What was said was obvious, there would be no battle! Man is the high point of creation and angels only messengers. End of story!

God withdrew partially and the angels have driven away to occupy their righteous places in the realms. Just me and my guardian. Catching me in the lap, he flies fast. Personally, I'll pass through the doors in a total of seven. In the end, the angel leaves me. Unlocking the last door, I have access to a new environment. To my surprise, I'm back in the room, meeting the master.

With a curious face, he resumes the conversation immediately.

"Did it work out, son of God? (Healer)

"Yes. It was really an incredible and unique experience. What now? What's the next step?

"Now the big moment has come. Wait a minute! (Healer)

He walked away a little and opened the bedroom door. Shaking his hair, screaming, "Renato, come here." In a few moments, he answers the call and enters the room. The door is locked again and there's the three of us, the three Musketeers. The master signals, we hold hands and form a circle. He starts to guide us.

"We are ready to begin a great journey that defies space and time. First, we must concentrate on our inner self, fixing the thought of an important fact of our life. When we reach the full concentration, we can walk meritoriously through the timeline and existence. However, we must be cautious not to alter the order of the facts.

"I get it. Something like the trip we've made in the past. (CLICKS THE PINTER)

"Can we get started? (Renato)

"Yes. (The healer)

Following the master's guidance, we begin the ritual of time passage. Every moment of this job, we discover a new world in ourselves. Instantly, our spirits and bodies tremble with emotion when they have access to the line of existence. Without fear, I string back time and my distressed spirit begins to penetrate a whole new world.

End